My Autumn Book

Wong Herbert Yee

Christy Ottaviano Books

Henry Holt and Company 🍁 New York

The air is crisp.

The sky turns gray.

Is autumn really on the way?

Downstairs I rush.

I can hardly wait,

To go outside and investigate.

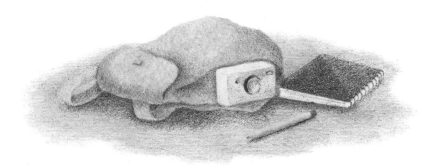

In a corner of the garden shed,
Spider spins a silken thread.
Hello, Spider!
What are you weaving?
Is it true that summer
Is leaving?

Crickets chirruping in the clover . . .
Another sign that warm days are over.

A chilly wind blows. I zip my jacket.
From the treetops I hear a racket.

The buzzing gets louder. It fills the air.
Cicada is warning us: Better beware!

Summer is leaving! Autumn coming!
Woodpecker agrees, *rap-a-tap* drumming.

Chipmunk scampers past,
Seeds packed in its cheeks,
Finding food for the upcoming weeks.

Squirrel digs a hole to bury its treasure.

Squirrel is expecting a change in the weather.

Caterpillar knows it's time to cocoon.

Ker-YAK! Blue Jay cries.

Autumn so soon?

Geese honk above,

Fly south in formation.

Trees dressing up for the fall celebration.

Dogwood shows off
A new crimson gown.

Oak changes into
A suit of rust brown.

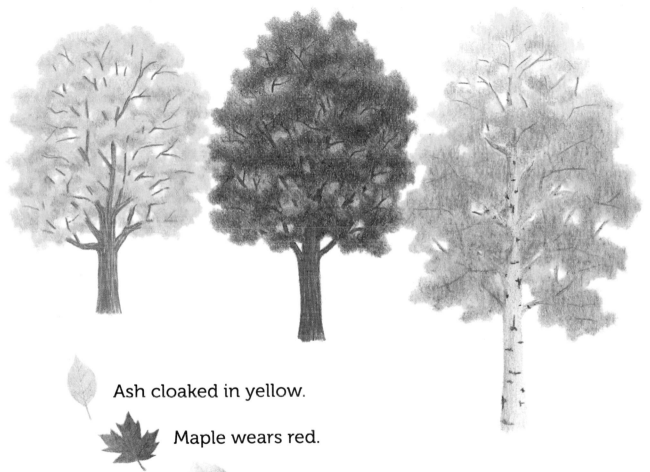

Ash cloaked in yellow.

Maple wears red.

Aspen, a crown of gold on its head.

Together they whisper and sway in the breeze,
Shaking loose acorns and batches of leaves.
Swirling and twirling, leaves spinning round,
A whirlwind of color that blankets the ground.

I search high and low,
Find one of each—
A ginkgo, a willow,
An elm, birch, and beech.

Summer is leaving, fall's on its way.
The seasons are changing,
No time to delay.

I dash up to my room
And open the door.

Empty my pack,

Spread things on the floor.

I find a jar for the acorns . . .

Fetch scissors and glue—
A pad of paper,
And crayons, too.

I decorate pages,

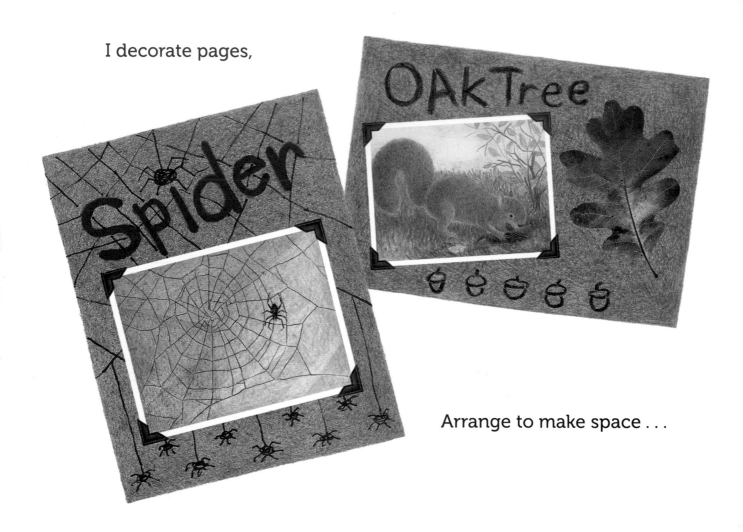

Arrange to make space . . .

There, it's all done!

Everything is in place.

When crickets no longer sing late at night

And the world outside

Has turned cold, black and white . . .

. . . I'll lie by the fire

With my book and remember,

Until autumn returns

Once more in September.

For Chase, Benaiah, and Luna

Henry Holt and Company, LLC
Publishers since 1866
175 Fifth Avenue
New York, New York 10010
mackids.com

Yee, Wong Herbert, author, illustrator.
My autumn book / Wong Herbert Yee.—First edition.
pages   cm
"Christy Ottaviano Books."
Summary: A young girl rushes outside when the air is crisp and the sky turns gray to
observe all of the changes that autumn brings.
ISBN 978-0-8050-9922-5 (hardback)
[1. Stories in rhyme. 2. Autumn—Fiction. 3. Nature study—Fiction.] I. Title.
PZ8.3.Y42My 2015   [E]—dc23   2014041426

Henry Holt books may be purchased for business or promotional use.
For information on bulk purchases, please contact the Macmillan Corporate and
Premium Sales Department at (800) 221-7945 x5442 or by e-mail at
specialmarkets@macmillan.com.

First Edition—2015 / Designed by Véronique Lefèvre Sweet
Prismacolors on Arches watercolor paper were used to create the illustrations
for this book.

Printed in China by Toppan Leefung Printing Ltd., Dongguan City,
Guangdong Province

10 9 8 7 6 5 4 3 2 1